Tutoring
CENTER

ABRA**X**US TASKER COLLEGE
SOPHMORE YEAR

Tutoring CENTER

Ali Whippe

4 Horsemen
Publications, Inc.

Tutoring Center

4 Horsemen Publications, Inc.
1497 Main St. Suite 169
Dunedin, FL 34698
4horsemenpublications.com
info@4horsemenpublications.com

Cover & Typesetting by Battle Goddess Productions

Ebook ISBN: 978-1-64450-050-7

Paperback ISBN: 978-1-64450-091-0

Audiobook ISBN: 978-1-64450-049-1

DEDICATION

To J, FOR THE NAUGHTY DREAM

TABLE OF CONTENTS

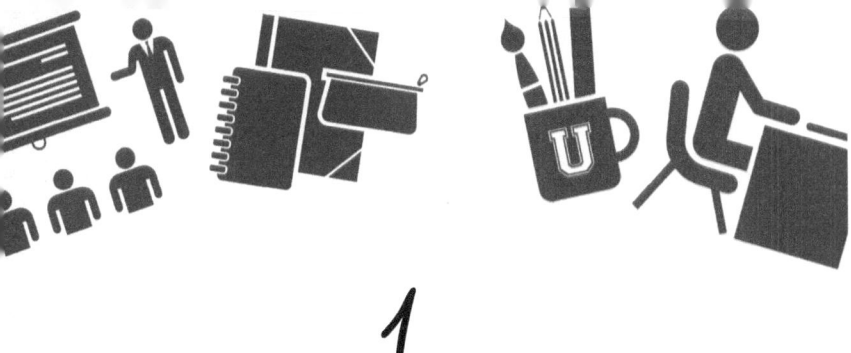

1

*W*illiam Tucker leaves the office of Dr. Jacoby, trying to hide his semi-erection with his book bag as he walks down the corridor, relieved that no other students are around. It's early evening, and the building is often empty at this time. Only professors are still lingering in their offices, catching up on grading or whatever else it is they do when they aren't teaching.

He tries to ignore the image that forms in his mind of Dr. Jacoby alone in her office after hours, hair unbound and free as she stretches in her desk chair, the shape of her full breasts revealed as her shirt tightens, long shapely legs on display as she rests her bare feet on the desk in front of her. He knows that she has started wearing stockings lately, likely garters if the quick glimpse he'd seen when he'd once walked into her office unannounced to find her slightly sprawled in the chair before she quickly rearranged her legs to hide her thighs was accurate, but at the start of the semester, she'd been prone to bare legs, and he knows she takes her shoes off under the desk every chance she gets.

He likes Dr. Jacoby, but it's an idle fantasy—she's never looked at him with true desire. He has a feeling that she has a lover and a truly wild side, but it's mostly conjecture, and though he enjoys toying with the idea, he enjoys his discussions with her far more. His slightly hard dick is more a result of the lack of action lately than any actual lust.

Reaching the end of the hallway, William looks from the door to the stairwell on his right to the elevator doors on his left. He can take the elevator down the four floors to the ground, but he's heard that alarm go off more than once while in class, and he's also heard his fellow students complain about how often it breaks down—and just how long it has taken for someone to show up and open those doors. He shivers at the thought of being stuck in there all night long.

Unless Dr. Jacoby discovered him and he hit the porn lottery, it would be a lonely experience. Though he has never had sex in an elevator before, he tries to shut down the part of his mind that wonders at the logistics. There was that bar that ran around the inside about hip level—could he wedge her on top of that and stand up? He might be the right height, but he doesn't want to end up doing the splits while fucking her—his thighs aren't up to that kind of exercise for any extended period of time. He's not in awful shape, but he's no athlete either. He doesn't want to lay her on the floor either, not after so many people have been doing who-knows-what in there all day. The idea of sitting naked on the floor douses any remaining desire, and he lets his mind wander in another direction.

He wonders who would miss him if he didn't go home tonight, and then tries not to think about that either. He pictures the empty apartment waiting for him and decides that he can't face it right now. Not yet. He's been lingering in his professor's office, finding reasons to stay and chat so he doesn't have to think about the empty side of the closet where all of his ex's clothes used to hang, the empty spaces in his bathroom where she used to keep all of her stuff. And how much stuff it had been—who knew how much shit women needed to get ready?

He decides that he doesn't mind having his bathroom sink to himself again. The rest, though, still stings.

I can't go home right now, William decides, checking his watch to see if the library is still open. 7:30. Another half hour. That will work for a bit, he decides, and then maybe he will go to the diner across the street and do some classwork until he gets tired and can't think anymore.

Plan in mind, he heads down the stairs, trotting down all four flights easily, his boots echoing loudly in the empty stairwell. He reaches the bottom, erection forgotten, mind already cataloguing the chapters he will read first, and opens the heavy outside door to the breezeway between this building and the library when he collides with another person. There is a crash of bodies, a flutter of papers and books that scatter around them, and a decidedly frustrated female curse.

William looks up, taking in the flowered dress surrounding luscious curves, the horn-rimmed glasses before bright eyes, the dark hair secured in a bun but with wisps escaping to frame a lovely face. "I'm so sorry!" he exclaims, pushing the door out again as it starts to close on both of them. "I didn't see you," he adds lamely.

The woman looks at him, then at the pile of papers and books laying haphazardly around them. One of the pages starts to blow away in the breeze from the open door, and without thinking, William steps on it to keep it in place. She sighs, the sound an echo of the tiredness in William's soul, and he grins at her in understanding. He is mildly surprised when she grins back. His experiences with women have taught him to expect annoyance or frustration—definitely not this shared camaraderie.

"No worries," she says in a friendly voice, pushing by him and allowing the door to close. She leans down to start gathering the papers and books, and William bends down to help. He moves his foot off the piece of paper and reaches down, and as he does, she leans forward, and the two of them clunk foreheads with a loud hollow sound.

The collision causes both of them to sit back hard on their heels and eventually fall onto their butts. William's first impulse is to laugh, and the sound escapes him without warning, but then she is laughing, and then they are staring at each other through a haze of pain and tears as the laughter tears through them. When they finally collect themselves, William is trying not to be so obvious in checking out the length of pale thigh exposed by her dress, the floral material currently riding high on her lap. She seems to follow his gaze, but instead of glaring at him, she smiles, the expression warming her face and matching her cheeks, still pink from laughter.

They sit there for another companionable moment, and then she sighs heavily, the sound loud in the empty stairwell, surveying the mass of paper and books around them. "Let me help you with that," William offers, reaching out slowly to collect the closest papers. He glances at them as he does so, surprised to discover they are not student essays as he had thought. The writing is double-spaced, but there are no headings to mark student names. A line from the text jumps out at him:

"Please," she screamed, "Please fuck me!"

Intrigued, William lets his eyes wander along the page, at first sure he is tired and misreading things, but then she is grabbing for the pages, and their hands meet, and she is looking at him and he is looking at her, each waiting for the other to speak. William takes the plunge.

"Interesting reading material," he comments, sliding the pages into a pile without reading further.

She quirks an eyebrow at him, again, not the expected reaction. If he'd been reading porn and someone busted him, he did not think he'd be able to sit there so calmly. She shrugs, one delicate shoulder raising, her flowered dress tightening against the line of her breast, her white sweater lifting and falling with a soft whisper of sound. "It gets boring just sitting there. I thought I'd spice it up."

He hands her the pile, noticing how her fingers trail along his as she takes it from him, then stacks it on top of one of the books she has gathered. "Sitting where?" he asks, hoping the moment will last, wishing to spend more time with this curious creature sitting across from him.

She gives him a considering look, and he sees the moment when she decides to trust him. "The Tutoring Center," she says. "It's a ghost town over there after 5 o'clock. I mostly just sit and read all evening."

"Really?" William asks. "I've seen some people over there at night..." He trails off, berating himself for contradicting her. She works there, he tells himself, surely she knows better than he does.

Again, that shrug. "Sometimes, sure, especially the football team around midterms, but right now? Dead zone." She scoots back, preparing to stand up. "I need something to read or I will fall asleep."

"Do you always read...such material?" he asks.

She gives him a naughty grin, a look all promise that makes him want to see her with her hair down, with that sweater on the floor, with that dress around her waist. "Sometimes," she replies. "A girl has to keep herself entertained."

"I would love to entertain you," he says, the words out before he can stop them, and he stares at her, thinking that surely he has gone too far, that she will call him a creep and walk away.

But the tutor does none of those things. Instead, she looks excited, eyes wide, breath slightly fast, a slow flush of red creeping up her chest. "How would you entertain me?" she breathes, and then he is crawling toward her, fallen books forgotten, and he lifts one of her hands from the pile she holds, raises it to his lips in an oddly gallant gesture, and releases it.

"Believe me," he tells her, "I could think of a few things."

She looks from her hand to his mouth and back again, and William knows she was expecting him to kiss her just then. She doesn't try to run away, a good sign, but he doesn't want to push it too far right now. But then, she speaks, and his doubts fade away.

"Would you show me some of those things?" she asks, moving to her knees and creeping closer, scattered papers forgotten beneath her. William doesn't miss the invitation in her voice.

"Oh yes," he promises, reaching for her hand again. "First," he says, "I would take your hand and kiss it." His lips are soft against her palm as he kisses it, his breath warm against her skin as he speaks, "And then I would move up your arm, tasting your skin." She shivers as he does as he says, his mouth moving slowly up the inside of her arm, soft butterfly kisses on the inside of her wrist and then up to her elbow as he pushes her sweater up before him.

She sighs, skin prickling in response to his touch. Moving his face away from her arm, he slowly reaches for her neck, sliding the sweater down off her shoulder so it hangs on her elbow and around her back.

"Then I would kiss you here," he announces, moving in slowly to trace his mouth along the line of her neck and shoulder, crossing the thin material of her dress's shoulder strap, noting that she isn't wearing a bra underneath, or if she is, it does not have straps. He slides his other hand up her opposite side under her sweater, pausing to stroke the sensitive skin near her breasts through the thin fabric of her dress, "And I would touch you there."

A breathy sound escapes her as his mouth reaches the top of her arm and his hand reaches up to stroke the curve of her breast. He pauses, enjoying the sensations, letting the moment linger, then pulls slowly away from her shoulder, leaving his hand resting under her breast. "And then I would pause, to see what you wanted next."

She is looking at him, something between wonder and desire in her expression, and William smiles at her. He knows that his methods of seduction aren't for everyone, but this woman seems to be enjoying everything.

"Next," she says, the word shaping her lips as she purses them for the sound, "you want to know what I want." Her eyes scan his face, lingering on his mouth. "I want you to tell me more."

He smiles at her, eyes narrowing playfully, and he leans forward again, left hand moving up to cover her breast, fingers circling her nipple, feeling it harden beneath his touch, "I would touch you here, loving the feel of you." He runs his other hand over her right shoulder, fingers sliding the strap of her dress down over her arm, the front of the dress following. His left hand abandons her nipple for a moment, mimicking the movement of his right hand and sliding her sweater and strap down to the crook of her elbow.

"And then I would admire your breasts," he narrates, gently tugging the forgiving material of the dress down and scooping out both of her breasts so they rest on top of the former neckline. He bends down to take a nipple in his mouth, and she gasps, leaning back and bracing herself with her palms on the floor behind her. "I would suck your nipples," he breathes against her, the warmth of his breath teasing her wet skin and causing her nipples to harden even more.

"Yes," she moans, lifting one hand to press his head against her breasts, fingers twining in his hair. He sucks for a long moment, moving from one nipple to the other, dexterous fingers replacing his mouth and stroking her sensitive skin. Her hands tighten in his hair, and she tugs him away, eyes dark with desire. "Then what?" she asks, voice undercut with a hint of command.

He pushes her back gently, his legs prodding between her thighs as he inches forward on his knees. She obliges, opening her legs to let him between them, but also scooting slowly backwards. "Then I would kiss you," he tells her, one hand still on her body as he moves her across the floor, the other sliding up her arm to her neck and in her hair, his face even with hers as his lips meet hers in a soft kiss. He is gentle, but firm, lips moving against hers in a way that is all promise.

When she opens her mouth, his tongue slides against hers, taking in her warmth and lingering in all the right places. The hand on her body holds her close, his knees still inching her backwards, and then her feet hit something. She opens her eyes, seeming surprised to see the bottom step behind her as she glances back. William uses the momentary distraction to put both hands on her hips and lift her onto the step. He scoots in close, kissing her again, both hands exploring the curves of her body, the soft material of her dress tantalizing under his fingers.

When they pause for breath, he lifts her up again, this time moving her up two steps, so she is sitting above him. "Then I would touch your thighs," he tells her, moving his hands to the outside of her thighs, slipping under her dress and scooting the material up. Her legs are lovely, smooth and toned, and she shivers as he reaches the top, hands cradling her hips, the flowered dress bunched up to reveal white cotton panties.

She leans back, elbows on the step behind her, and looks down the length of her body at him, her exposed breasts resting on top of the dress, nipples hard.

"And then I would want to see all of you," he explains, "so I would slide these off." His fingers begin the agonizingly slow work of removing her panties. She watches him as her flesh is revealed, breasts heaving as she breathes, a flush working its way up her neck. He tugs the panties down and over the white sandals, then tucks them into his pocket, not wanting to put them on the floor of the stairwell. He touches her feet, then runs his hands up her calves, dipping behind her knees and then between her thighs, spreading them apart as he leans forward even more.

"I would watch your face as I touched you," he says as his hands slide across her skin, "here," and then as his thumb reaches the swollen nub of her clit, "and here."

She gasps, head falling back as he gently presses, then she is looking at him, biting her lower lip as he strokes her skin, slow luscious circles with his thumb, and then his other hand is sliding lower, fingers tracing the edges of her smooth skin before sliding slowly inside her, her warm wetness plump with desire. Her eyes narrow in pleasure, but she doesn't look away, doesn't lose herself in the sensation yet. William's hands continue to move in a slow delicious rhythm, and her hips begin to move against him, gently urging him along.

"I would want to see you come for me," he says, thumb moving faster against her clit, and she rocks herself against him, a low moan spilling from her lips. "So I would rub right there," he describes, "and press here," as his hands move in tandem, her hips moving faster against him, her breasts bouncing as she slides closer to orgasm.

"Will you come for me?" he asks, and then he is up on his knees again, lips finding hers without losing the rhythm of both

9

hands, and as his tongue finds hers, she shudders against him, a moan lost inside his mouth, and he lets his hands slow, but does not move them away. "Yes," he whispers against her open mouth, "that's what I would do." He moves his face away for a moment, allowing her to catch her breath, then adds, "But I would not be finished after one orgasm."

She regains her breath and her composure, her expression satisfied but curious. "No?" she asks, a hand brushing loose strands of hair out of her face, her bun coming loose. "What would you do next?"

He leans back, then scoots down, sitting on his folded legs, and slowly moves his hands around, enjoying the small gasps of pleasure escaping her. He settles his face against her knee, kissing the skin of her inner thigh, then moving up.

"I would need to know what you taste like," he says, using both hands to press her thighs wide, "so I would kiss you here." He presses his lips to her clit, sucking quickly and releasing her as her hips jerk forward. One hand slides down and slips inside her again, not moving, but pressing against her from the inside.

"Then I would want to feel you," he whispers against her skin, "and lick you." His tongue runs along the length of her, starting near his finger inside her and ending on her clit and lingering. She shudders against him, and his other hand reaches around her hips and settles under her ass, holding her steady so she can't move too far from him.

"I would want to hear what you want," he orders, then licks her again, finger joined by another inside her as he starts another slow rhythm.

She says nothing for a moment, but then he pauses, looking up at her. His tongue darts out for a quick lick, then retreats. "I would want to know if you wanted me to do this," a longer luscious lick from top to bottom, "or this," and a final long suck that has her head sink limply back and her thighs begin to tremble, "or maybe this."

"Yes," she breathes.

Another long suckling where his tongue presses hard against her as his fingers continue to move inside her. "Yes what?"

"Yes that!" she says, voice slightly louder. "That is so fucking good!"

"What is so fucking good?" he asks, warm breath close, fingers still moving in that maddening rhythm. "Tell me."

"I want you to suck my clit!" she semi-yells, the words echoing in the empty stairwell. "Then I want you to fuck me!"

"Fuck you?" he asks, sucking her again until she shudders. "How will I fuck you?" He sucks again, fingers sliding in and out of her, and her hips are pumping up and down on his hand. "Tell me how!"

"Hard!" she yells, body lost in pleasure as she rocks on his hand, and he sucks again, this time not releasing her until she tenses, entire body taut with the power of her orgasm. "Fuck me hard," she moans as she comes, "make me come on your dick. I need you inside of me!"

She falls back, collapsing on the stairs, and he uses the moment to remove his hands, unzipping his pants and pulling out his hard cock. He sits up, knees still on the ground but his body even with hers, pressing the tip of his cock against her wet opening. "Look at me," he commands. "I want you to watch me fuck you."

Her eyes open slowly, and her head comes back up, but then is looking at his cock in his hand pressed between her thighs, and she bites her lip again, and her body slides down a little, eager to have him inside of her. "You want this cock?" he asks, rubbing himself against her, her wetness combining with his pre-cum to create delightful friction. "You want this inside you?"

"Yes!" she says, one arm reaching forward to grab him, pressing herself forward. "I want you inside me!" Her hand reaches behind him as she sits up slightly, fingers grabbing his ass and pulling him closer.

He allows himself to be moved, the tip of his cock sliding into that delicious warmth. He pauses, then pulls back, slipping in and out slowly. "Like that?" he asks, one hand grabbing her hip and holding her where he wants her, the other reaching up to caress her breast, rubbing her nipple with his thumb.

The hand on his ass tightens, and then she is sitting up on the step, her other hand grabbing his hips, and she presses herself onto him, his cock sliding in deep. She sighs, "Fuck yes," and scoots forward, trying to get traction, her legs wrapping around his hips and tugging him closer. He leans toward her, capturing her mouth with his, letting her taste herself on his lips, her tongue pressing into his mouth as he slides his hips slowly back and forth. "More," she pleads into his mouth. "I need more!"

His hand abandons her breast, joining the other on her hips, and he tugs her close, giving her the connection she wants. Now more balanced, she presses herself into him, and he grips her hips hard, yanking her against him, his cock plunging deep inside her warmth. "Yes!" she yells.

He moves her again, using his position to tuck himself underneath her, his hands rocking her hips as he dives in and out of her. He feels her start to tighten even more around his cock, "And then I would watch you come on my cock!" he yells, and she opens her eyes as she comes, body shuddering in ecstacy.

After a moment, she slows her movement, some of the desperation leaving her, and a new wildness seems to fill her. She sits up, allowing his cock to retreat a little, then releases her legs from his hips.

"And then I would make you sit down," she tells him, pulling away and scooting aside so that he can sit on the vacated step. He does so, turning around so he sits on the step instead of her. "And I would take these off," she says, kneeling before him to tug off his pants and boxers. They tangle around his ankles, but she doesn't try to get them passed his boots, leaving them there and standing up, glorious body before him as she turns around, shucking off the forgotten sweater in one angry motion and lowering herself onto him, her legs pressing his knees together as she sits on his lap, her back to him. He leans back on the step, resting on his elbows as she did before, then watches as she lowers a most perfect ass before his sight, her warmth embracing his hard cock as she takes him inside, and after a moment where she adjusts her feet on either side of him, and presses her hands against the tops of his thighs for balance, she lifts herself slowly up and down on him.

"And then I would ride his cock until I came again!" she says, the words triumphant as she finds her rhythm, beautiful ass pounding up and down as she moves. William is enthralled, but doesn't want to lose himself in the moment, not yet, so he reaches up with one hand and grips her hip, following the rhythm she sets for a moment, before sliding his hand around and down to stroke her clit with his thumb.

"And I would rub that sweet clit until you came on my cock," he groans, trying to slow the inexorable build of pleasure spiking through him. "Come for me, baby," he demands, "Come now!"

He rubs harder, faster, and she shudders on him, hands gripping his thighs in spasms as the orgasm rocks her. She slumps then, leaning back against him, gasping for breath, sweat coating her neck. He sits up, pressing her back to him, and uses the break to slide her dress up and over her head. She allows the movement, hand reaching up lazily to adjust her glasses where they are askew on her face, resting limply against him, and then

13

he is rubbing her breasts, slowly, but determined, and she moves, the slight motion pressing him deep inside her again as her muscles relax. His hands wander down, and he reaches her clit again, exerting gentle pressure when she stiffens against him, clearly needing a moment, and slipping down to feel himself inside of her. She shudders, a low spasm of pleasure, as his fingers caress her skin around his cock, and then he is kissing her neck. She turns her head, and then she is kissing him, and she moves ever so gently, rocking slowly up and down on his cock.

"Then I would fuck you slow until you screamed my name," he says against her lips, and she pauses, eyes opening to look at him.

"But I don't know your name," she says, a bit of a giggle escaping as she moved up and down on his cock.

"William Turner," he growls, and moves both hands to her hips to keep her moving at the current rhythm, pleasure building again inside him, and this time he doesn't want to stop, "and don't you ever forget it."

She moves on him faster, still not the frantic rhythm of a few moments before, but definitely on her way to another orgasm. "I will never forget your name, William Turner," she moans, eyes closing as the pleasure builds in her.

"And your name?" he asks, trying to slow the moment, but aware that he is going to lose himself and soon. Slow steady rhythms always undo him. "What name will I dream about tonight?"

"Kimberly," she answers, then kisses him again, slow and languorous. "Kimberly Chapman."

His hands press hard against her hips, setting the rhythm, "I would tell you how lovely you are, Kimberly Chapman," he says, loving the feel of her name on his lips, and then she kisses him again, both of them lost in pleasure.

William is about to lose himself completely, but a sound echoes through his concentration, breaking his rhythm and coordination, and he opens his eyes to meet Kimberly's stunned expression as her brain processes the noise. The door has opened in the stairwell, probably not on the second floor because it sounds father away, but definitely marking the arrival of someone else in the building.

Kimberly stands up quickly, reaching for her discarded dress and sweater and clutching them to her chest, eyes wide and hair wild as she takes in the sprawl of papers and books abandoned on the floor. William stands, nearly tumbles as his pants catch around his ankles, and then yanks them up awkwardly. Kimberly bends down and starts collecting the papers, but William stops her with a gesture, motioning to the books instead. She begins gathering them, deciding to abandon the pages, and William helps, clutching three books against his chest with one hand and the other holding his pants up. She looks at the door, then down at her clothes, and he can see the indecision in her eyes.

It's one thing to abandon papers with no names on it; it's another to run outside completely naked. It's late in the evening, but the college isn't completely deserted.

William makes a snap decision, gestures for her to follow, and darts farther into the stairwell, ducking underneath the space created by the stairs. Most of the school stairwells use the space for storage, and this stairwell is no exception, the space occupied with blue gym mats stacked both horizontally and vertically. There is a space against the wall wide enough for them to fit inside, and William shoos Kimberly in ahead of him, using his body to block the opening in case the person decides to come back here. Kimberly lets the books in one hand tumble to the surface of a pile of horizontal mats about chest high, the sound a low thud that seems very loud in the echoing stairwell, and William sets his down with more grace. She is tugging her dress over her head, arms akimbo as the twisted material gets stuck, and he reaches out to help her. Both of them freeze as they hear footsteps on the stairs above their heads. Without thought, he lifts her up onto the mats and scoots up behind her.

They hear a soft curse in Spanish as the person comes down the stairs, no doubt taking in the spray of abandoned papers, and then there is some shuffling. William wonders if it could be the janitor; he doesn't think another student would bother to pick up the papers.

Kimberly is kneeling in front of him, head barely peeking over the vertical mats piled in front of the ones they are on, her body faintly outlined in the dim light, and William can't help the way his dick hardens again, danger momentarily forgotten. Her head cocks to the side, hair mussed and bun lost as she listens to the person on the other side of the steps.

The shuffling sounds continue for a moment, and William scoots closer to her, allowing his pants to fall down around his thighs as he presses himself against her. She gasps, and there is a pause in the sounds outside, then her hands are reaching behind her, fingers grabbing his hard cock and pressing it. She turns around, her mouth open in shock but something naughty crossing her face. William moves his hips forward, cock angling for her opening, and she grins at him over her shoulder, opening her legs to let him in.

He hovers at her entrance for a moment, straining to hear the person on the other side of the stairs, but also so blue-balled that he really doesn't care much about what they do over there. The shuffling continues, papers being collected, and he inches forward, cock slipping inside of velvety heat one slow inch at a time. Kimberly lets out a slow ragged breath, and reaches back to grab his hand where it rests on her ass. He pulls out slowly, letting the friction build, and then slides back inside. Her other hand reaches around behind her, and then she is gripping both of his hands where they hold her ass, letting him set the rhythm.

He moves a few more times, tension building, and the person continues to collect papers. There is more shuffling, the sound of a random pile of papers being tapped into a pile, and then a cough and another Spanish curse.

William pauses, wondering if the person had heard them, but then there is a soft chuckle from the other side of the stairs, and more shuffling as the person rearranged the papers. A soft thud lets them know that the newcomer has decided to sit down on the stairs, a soft sliding of paper against paper letting them know the person is reading the discarded papers. William holds in a laugh, unable to quite believe the situation. An hour ago, he never would have guessed that he'd be hiding under a staircase with his dick buried in the hottest woman he'd ever met with a stranger reading porn a few feet away.

He allows himself to move again, ever so slowly, and Kimberly moves with him, as caught up in the moment as he is. A few more soft strokes, and then there is a chuckle from the stranger. He doesn't pause, the slow motion of his cock inside her sweet pussy driving him mad. Another few chuckles, and then another sound, one he recognizes, an intrigued noise.

There is another shift as the newcomer turns to the next page, and then the unmistakable sound of a zipper. William doesn't stop, but doesn't speed up either, knowing both he and Kimberly are intently listening to the stranger on the steps. More paper shuffling, and then something that could be clothing shuffling, and then the unmistakable slow fapping sound of a man masturbating. Kimberly doesn't turn around, and William is grateful for that, knowing they would both lose it if they looked at one another right now. Instead he continues to slowly slide in and out of her, careful not to move too quickly so their bodies don't make any noise.

Kimberly is so wet and tight that he knows he isn't going to last much longer. The sound of the fapping gets more intense, and they can hear labored breathing as another paper shuffles. Then, there is a moan, and a hand slaps against the stairs above them, and Kimberly's pussy squeezes tight around him, her body shuddering. William's entire body convulses, and he comes, not hard as he had first imagined, but slow and agonizing and sweet, pumping at the same speed a few more times until the moment passes, and he falls back on his haunches, Kimberly following him to sit on his lap, his cock still buried inside of her.

William takes long slow breaths, feeling his heart pounding in his head, the feeling oddly echoed by Kimberly's own pulse beating against him as she sprawls against him. They don't move, listening for the newcomer.

After a moment, the breathing slows, and then there is the shuffling of clothing and the zipper again. The papers are shuffled, there is a cough, and then the exterior door opens and footsteps walk through. The door bangs shut, and Kimberly turns in the circle of William's arms, staring at him. They both look at one another for a long moment, and then dissolve into fits of wheezing giggles, the movement pushing him out of her as he body tightens.

When they have calmed down a little bit, Kimberly scoots away, rolling over the sit on the mat a foot away from him. "Well," she says finally, "that was definitely entertaining."

Williams grins at her, then scoots to the edge of the mat and slides his pants back up as he jumps off, taking the time to actually zip and button them before reaching out a hand to help Kimberly climb down. They both grab her books, and creep out from behind the mats.

William holds her books as she shrugs into her sweater and rearranges her hair, massing it back into a bun in a way that makes William want to take it down again. She gives him a look as if asking how she looks, and he nods at her. She looks wonderful, skin rosy with the aftereffects of good sex, and now that he knows what is underneath that dress, he is tempted to take it off of her again.

He looks around at the stairwell, then down at himself. She considers, then steps forward and smooths his hair before she nods, giving him the same approval to go out in public. She lands a soft kiss on his lips that turns into something more, and they linger there in the stairwell next to the mats, not caring if someone walks in on them kissing.

After a long moment, they pause, and Kimberly looks at him. "What do you say we go grab a cup of coffee and get to know one another? It's far too early to go home yet."

William nods. "I know a great diner right around the corner."

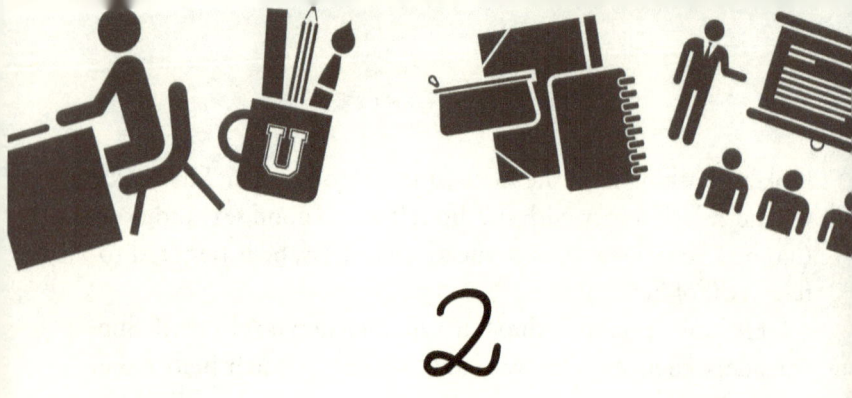

2

"Are you a writer, William?" Kimberly asks, eyes dark and inviting over the mug of coffee. They have been talking for about an hour, getting to know one another in other ways.

He shrugs, looking at his own empty mug on the table, then decides to own it. She could hardly be surprised, given the way he had just made love to her. She had to know he loved words. "Yeah," he admits, then remembers her voice shouting in the stairwell, body flushed with desire for him, and says it again, stronger this time. "Yes, I'm a writer."

"What do you write?" she asks, her voice a low purr.

He shrugs again, then looks down again, knowing what he should expect her expression to do when he says it, knowing how women normally respond to him, but hoping this time will be different, that she will be different. She already is different. He tries to shake the nagging sense of inevitability that lingers. Kimberly isn't like the other women he's known. She isn't going to react the way he expects. "I write about...life," he admits.

She leans in, face curious, and a rush of excitement fills William's chest. "What about life?" The words are nearly a whisper now. "Do you write about what just happened?"

"Not usually," he tells her, thinking about his few attempts at erotica, "but I could write something for you." He looks up, thinking of her alone in the Tutoring Center after hours, reading his words. "Just for you." He cocks his head, biting his lower lip. "Would you read it?"

She considers, a small smile playing on her lips. "That depends. Would it be worth reading?"

He nods, and confidence fills him. He knows how to use words. "I think I could keep your attention," he teases. "Perhaps you'd enjoy it as much as the janitor." She giggles, and he reaches out to take her hand. "What kind of story would you like to read?"

She ponders for a moment, then tilts her head, bun gone, all that long dark hair sliding over her shoulders and caressing her upper arms, bare now that she's removed her sweater. "How about a story about life?" she replies with a smirk.

"Life," he repeats, ideas spinning in his head, "like real life.... or something else?"

She looks around, "Well, I have a real life, so something else would probably keep my attention more effectively," she breathes.

William nods, a plot already forming as he stares at her, taking in her small mannerisms, her gestures, her expressions. He knows he can capture her in fiction. "I can bring it to you tomorrow," he offers.

"Tomorrow night?" she clarifies. "I'm closing the Tutoring Center, so I'll be there alone after 6."

"Sounds perfect," he says.

"Awesome," she says, "now let's talk about my panties still in your pocket."

3

*W*illiam stands in front of the elevator with Kimberly, waiting for the doors to open. He is a little bit nervous to get in the contraption, especially considering what he knows about the elevator in the Humanities Building, but he's willing to risk it to spend a few more minutes with her.

Kimberly needs a few things from the Tutoring Center before she heads home for the night. She hadn't planned on leaving when she bumped into him in the stairwell; she had just been running over to the mailroom before heading back to the Tutoring Center. Now it is very late, and the Center is closed, so she has to remove the sign that she left hours earlier, the one that lied, saying "Be back in five minutes." She hopes no students waited for any real length of time. She really had meant to be right back; she hadn't expected to bump into William in the stairwell and get completely distracted.

"It's fine," she tells William as the doors slide open. "I use this elevator all the time."

"I know," William admits, but he can't shake the feeling he has that he is about to get stuck in an elevator.

She grabs his hand and leads him inside, leaning down to press the button for the fourth floor. The elevator moves slowly, but steadily up, each floor marked by a low ding. William is staring at the doors, face nervous, so Kimberly leans in to him, propping her books in one arm and tugging his face down to kiss her. He seems to enjoy the distraction, soft lips pressing against hers. He focuses, adjusting the books he carries for her so he has a free arm to wrap around her back, and runs a hand up her spine. She shivers in his embrace.

The elevator stops on the fourth floor with a ding, and the doors slide open. William finishes kissing her, and steps back, clearly expecting her to lead him out of the elevator, but instead, she takes the pile of books in his arm, adds it to her own, and places it in the corner. The doors stay open for a moment and then begin to slide shut. William starts to say something, but then Kimberly has both hands in his hair, tugging him down to kiss her again, and the words die on his tongue. Both of his hands come around her back and slide down to cup her ass, and she bites his lip a little.

The door has shut completely, but the elevator hasn't moved. William realizes that it won't move until someone else calls it to a different floor, or someone on the fourth floor pushes the button. He's seen the dark offices along the hallway leading to the library and he doesn't think anyone will be using this elevator any time soon.

Then again, he'd had the same thought about the stairs earlier tonight. But that had been a janitor. Not that janitors wouldn't use the elevator—they often do to move the carts—but anyone would have to call the elevator down to the bottom. It doesn't move fast; they will have a chance to get themselves presentable again.

Besides, Kimberly is pressing herself against him and he knows that she isn't wearing panties, and he slides his hands beneath her dress to feel the slick wetness between her thighs. She turns so her back is against the wall, and then he pushes himself against her, wondering just how he's going to fuck her in this elevator. He wants to speak, to say something, knowing that words turn her on, but there is an odd silence between them, a connection purely physical, and he just wants the moment to last.

Kimberly reaches down and starts undoing his pants, dextrous fingers unfastening the button and lowering the zipper, and then his hard cock is in her hands, and she is stroking him. She releases him for a moment, her hand slipping beneath her dress to touch her own wetness, and then she is sliding her smooth hands over his cock, the friction a promise of pleasures to come. He kisses her again, tugging her hair down and pressing her against the wall. There is a railing that runs around the middle of the elevator, and William wonders if she can rest on it to get her at a better angle.

She seems to read his mind because she hops up, resting the edge of her ass on the edge of the railing, and spreads her legs welcomingly. William presses himself between them, his weight holding her steady on the railing, a hand under her ass to hold her in place, and then her hand is guiding him into her wetness, the tip slipping inside and then she moans as he fills her completely, the sensation of warmth and tightness multiplied by the feeling of her fingers still wrapped around him, sliding up and down as he presses his length into her and rocks back out again. She uses her other hand to grip his shoulder hard, balancing against the wall and rocking softly up and down on his cock. Her legs wrap around his hips, urging him deeper.

He moans, setting a slow luscious pace, boots getting excellent traction on the elevator floor, and loses himself in the moment. The only sound is their panting breath, the noise of their bodies fitting together, a wet slapping that, after the evening filled with words, only turns him on more. Words are well and good, but there is something to be said for good old fashioned fucking. Kimberly's hand continues to slide against him as he fucks her, a lovely sensation against his cock, her fingers pressing against her clit in a rhythm that grows slightly faster as he moves. She moans, the sound lost in his mouth, and he devours her with his mouth, one hand holding her firmly under her ass and the other holding her chin as he rocks on his heels.

He speeds up, suddenly wanting to come again, and then she is biting his lips as she kisses him, her hand on his shoulder digging in as she moves faster, body pounding up and down harder, breasts bouncing wildly against his chest. He puts a hand against the wall to brace himself, fingers digging into her ass and putting her at the perfect angle, and then he lets go completely, pounding into her until the orgasm hits, letting his body freeze as he comes into her, then gasping in ragged breaths as she shudders against him, finding her own pleasure just before he steps back, light-headed and weak-kneed, and then she slides down off the railing onto shaky legs.

They both stand there for a moment, Kimberly gripping the railing behind her with both hands, gasping and flushed, and William leans back against the closed doors, heart pounding like mad and eyes glazed with the residue of lust. After a moment, William adjusts his pants, tucking himself back inside and zipping up. Kimberly's dress has already fallen back into place.

He follows her gaze as her eyes linger on his pocket, and he tucks the exposed edge of her panties back inside, shaking his head with a grin. She raises an eyebrow, but says nothing.

There is another long moment filled only with their slowing breaths, and then they look at one another again. Kimberly steps away from the wall and William steps away from the door, and they meet in the middle of the elevator for another kiss, lips moving slowly against one another, exploring, comforting, loving.

It is a long time before the elevator doors open again.

4

Kimberly Chapman waits in the Tutoring Center, trying not to watch the clock as the minutes tick by. The computer monitor before her is loaded with numbers, formulas she should be reviewing since the football team would be in tomorrow to prepare for their algebra midterm, but Kimberly doesn't need to study; she could tutor algebra in her sleep. But the numbers have been a distraction, and one her boss would approve of, if Dianne Carver ever actually came in the Center at night. But no one has even been there to see her fake brushing up, and now she gives up completely.

The clock says 5:58. She wonders how prompt William Turner will be, excited by the thought of seeing him, of hopefully getting to slide that glorious cock inside her again, intrigued by the story he had promised to write her. Her hand slides down the black dress she wears, lingers on her knee, and then wanders underneath the dress and slides along her inner thigh. Thoughts of William's words, then his mouth on her, then his cock inside her, the rush of the frantic elevator sex, and soon she is stroking herself, finger deftly rubbing her clit, glad she left the panties at home today.

She watches the glass doorway between this room and the hallway, knowing that the library on the other end of the hallway still has clusters of students, but sure that none of them will come to the Center this late. She hadn't been kidding when she told William the place is a Dead Zone after five o'clock.

Her finger moves again at the thought of William, and she glances first at the clock and then at the door. It really wouldn't do to have him walk in on her fingering herself. Then again, she considers the look that would cross his face, and wonders what naughty words he would say, and her finger moves faster, low heat building in her belly.

Motion in the hallway catches her attention and she pulls her hand out from under her dress, sliding the chair forward so she is nearly under the desk, attention clearly focused on the monitor when the door opens.

William is just as handsome as he was the night before, his upper body covered by a button-down shirt that doesn't quite hide the definition of his muscles. He's not a large man, not at all, but he's fit and toned enough to make her want to run her hands along his chest, kissing her way down the muscles of his stomach and lower. He takes in the empty room and her desk in the far corner. Kimberly's face lights in a smile, and William returns the look.

"You looking for some help?" she asks jokingly.

"Maybe," he replies, crossing the room, walking passed computers and a few cubicles in the center to stand before her L-shaped desk. "I was told someone here might be looking for some entertainment."

Kimberly spins her chair slightly to face him directly and leans back. She watches William take in the simple black dress that can't hide her curves, the skirt modestly covering her knees and falling mid-calf but revealing the small black sandals on her feet. She lifts one leg and crosses it over the other, the motion hopefully slow enough for him to guess that she isn't wearing panties. "Maybe," she says. "Depends on what you mean by entertainment."

William grins as he watches her legs move. "Well, well," he observes in a low voice that sends a shiver across her skin, "you seem to have left some clothing at home today."

She nods, a smirk in her voice. "You wouldn't believe what happened."

"Try me," he says, putting down his bag on the chair and leaning on the edge of the desk.

She uncrosses her legs and spreads them, scooting the hem of the dress up her thighs. "Someone seems to have taken my panties," she says quietly, a little pout on her lips.

"Really? How upsetting," he comments, glancing out the glass door to the empty hallway beyond. He slides his legs up and over the desk, so he leans on her side now, and then he sinks to his knees before her chair. "I think I might have to investigate further."

"Would you?" she asks, and her legs open a little bit more. William scoots forward, accepting the invitation, and his hands slide up the outside of her thighs, causing chills to run through her at his touch. He pauses at her bare hips, then slides both hands lower and between her thighs, stroking the warm heat there. "And what do you think?" she asks, eyes dark with desire.

"I think I may have to explore the issue," he tells her, sinking down so he cannot be seen beneath the desk, and he tugs the chair toward him, burying his face between her thighs under her dress.

Kimberly gasps, pleasure flooding her as his mouth closes over her clit, tongue sucking in the way he knows she likes. One hand slips down to stroke her pussy low and slow, but the other creeps up underneath her dress to cup her breast, thumb sliding across the nipple. Kimberly whimpers, the sound loud in the empty room, and she watches the door, glad that no one is there. "Oh yes," she whispers, one hand pressing against the back of William's head under her dress, pushing him into her, and the other reaching up to caress her other breast, rubbing one nipple as he rubs the other. "You can keep exploring all day."

William reaches down and tugs her forward on the chair, exposing more of her flesh to his hands and mouth, and she puts both hands on the back of his head, forgetting about the glass door, forgetting about everything but the motion of his mouth on her skin, the pulsing building heat in her lower belly. Both of his hands slide between her legs, and his fingers begin that magical motion in conjunction with his tongue. Already excited from the few moments before he arrived, Kimberly comes quickly, the orgasm hard as her pulse echoes in her fingertips, her fingers white from where she's been pressing them against William's head. She releases him, letting her body slide down in the chair, pleasure rendering her muscles limp with fatigue.

William sits up, giving her space, and surveys her. "I've been waiting to taste you all day," he says, running a hand along his lips.

Regaining her head, Kimberly opens an eye. "I thought you were writing all day?"

He nods. "I was, and that's why I couldn't wait to see you." He climbs to his knees and stands up, easily sliding back over the desk to his bag. He opens it, then slides out a blue folder with a small stack of papers inside. He lays it on the desk, then slides it toward her.

"And in a folder!" she exclaims, eyes meeting his, no doubt recalling the explosion of loose papers that had brought them together in the stairwell. Kimberly leans forward to take it, smiling at him as she flips it open. She removes the pages and lays them on top of the folder, biting her lip as she begins to scan the words.

"Oh no," he says, and she pauses, looking up at him, eyes already hooded with desire. "Not like that," he tells her. "Read it out loud." He steps around the desk to stand behind her, warm hands running up her sides and leaning down to kiss her neck.

His hands move up her arms to her shoulders, and he tugs her hair out of the loose bun, letting the dark waves fall down her back. He pushes her hair to one side, continuing to kiss her skin.

She grins, leaning into his touch, then takes a breath before beginning.

"Kimberly sits in the desk chair in front of her computer. The room is empty, and her mind wanders to the exciting rendezvous from the night before."

She looks back at him with a grin and a quick kiss, tasting herself on his mouth, then glances back down.

"Recalling the touch of William's lips on her skin, she shivers, and her hand slides lazily down to stroke her side through the thin material of her flowered dress."

Kimberly glances down at the black dress she wears, but lets her hand slip down, all to aware of how much her actions mirror the few moments before William arrived.

William continues to kiss her neck, hands pressing close through the dress. "I didn't know what you would be wearing," he admits. "Though I did think you'd wear panties." His fingers slide over her ass, tracing the line where her panties would be. "I was looking forward to taking them off you again."

Kimberly shrugs, pressing herself against him, feeling the hardness of his cock against her back. "What can I say? Some guy left with them last night and never gave them back."

"Sounds like a real bastard," William comments, hands sliding the bottom of her dress up so he can caress the skin beneath.

Kimberly nods, her loose hair caressing her skin. "Oh yeah, but he fucked like a champion."

"Did he now?" William asks, fingers sliding between her thighs, stroking her clit with his thumb. "Did he fuck this pussy? Tell me more."

"I didn't know I could come so many times in a row," she tells him, her hand reaching down to rest on top of his, loving the feeling of his hands on her skin. "He just knew how to touch me in all the right places."

William nods, then plucks the folder from her hand, laying it on the desk in front of them and turns her around to face him and then pushes her gently back into the chair. "How did he touch you?" he whispers. "Show me those right places."

Her hand pushes the dress up, revealing her flushed skin, and her other hand grabs her breast, rubbing the nipple gently. "He rubbed my nipples," she says, mimicking the motion as she speaks, "and he kissed my clit."

"Show me," he repeats, cock hardening as he watches her fingers move down to slide along her clit. She can see the outline in his pants, and his voice has roughened.

She strokes the small nub, then drags her finger along the length of herself. "He had these wonderful fingers," she tells him, "and he knew just where to put them." She rubs herself again, short slow bursts that cause her toes to curl.

"And then he put his fingers inside me," she says, her fingers doing the same, disappearing into her pussy, but her thumb stays out and with a slight adjustment of her hand, starts to rub her clit while her fingers move in and out slowly.

"He made me so hot," she says, the motion of her hand increasing in speed and pressure, and her other hand squeezes her nipple hard and she gasps, closing her eyes in her pleasure.

"He made you come," William observes, voice low as his hand brushes against his cock. "Show me now. Show me how you came for him."

"Show me that cock," she says suddenly, eyes opening as she looks at him. "I want to see it again!"

"This cock?" William grins, hands quickly unzipping his pants and tugging himself free from both pants and boxers. He leaves both up on his hips, but strokes himself a few times, giving her an eyeful of his hard cock.

"Yes," she moans, hand moving faster. "I wanted him to fuck me with that cock." She licks her lips, eyes slitted with pleasure. "Will you fuck me with your cock?" she asks, and he strokes himself again, biting his lip as he watches her come, the orgasm shuddering through her.

He gives her a moment to recover, then leans forward to take her face in his hand. "Lovely," he says, then kisses her hard, lips demanding as she shudders in the chair before him, her hands reaching out to grab his cock, her fingers wrapping around his length and squeezing. She pushes him back on the desk, and scoots the chair forward, not letting go of him. He leans back on the desk, very aware of the glass door behind them, across the room, but still totally see-through if anyone were to approach. Kimberly grins up at him.

"No worries," she orders. "Anyone coming in would only see your back, and you'd just be sitting on the desk." She leans down to take his cock in her mouth, but not before adding, "Besides, no one comes in here at night."

William leans back as the warmth of her mouth encloses his cock. She takes him in deep, then slides back up, setting up a slow rhythm designed to break him. He moans, the sound escaping him in a long low rush, and she keeps up her pace, tongue swirling around the sensitive tip each time she pulls up, only to suck hard as she moves back down. Her hand cups his balls, fingers pressing the soft skin hard against him in the same rhythm. She doesn't speed up, knowing that she doesn't want him to come yet, but well aware of what her torturous speed is doing to him.

She remembers how he came the night before, quietly shuddering behind her as they hid from the janitor, and she decides that tonight will be different. She releases his cock from her mouth, replacing it with her hand slowly stroking him up and down, and she looks up at him.

"So, does your story include the couch in the back room?"

He jerks, eyes swiveling back to her as he tries to process what she said. "What back room?" he asks, brain finally understanding what she has said. She gestures with her eyes to the doorway in the middle of the back wall behind the desk. William follows her gaze, but he clearly hasn't realized that the door opens to an employee lounge.

She stands but doesn't release his cock from her grip. She moves, and he slides off the desk to follow. She walks him to the door, his hands holding his pants at his hips, and she puts in the code to open the door. The lock flashes green, and she pushes the handle down, opening the door and pulling him through. She walks him over to the small brown couch that sits against the back wall, then pushes him onto it, releasing his cock as he sits down hard.

"Wait here," she orders, then walks across the room and back out into the public part of the Tutoring Center. She walks to the glass door, makes sure that no one is walking down the hallway toward her, and flips the sign to say CLOSED. She turns off the light so the room goes dark, then navigates by the lights of the computers back to the desk. She collects the blue folder and William's bag, and heads back to the back room, entering the code again to unlock the door. William is sitting where she left him, and he notices the dark room behind her as the door swings shut again.

"Closing early?" he asks.

She nods. "Oh yes. It appears that something has come up that requires my immediate attention."

"What would that be?" he asks, leaning back into the couch cushions, hard cock standing proud from the tumble of his pants.

"I wanted to hear you this time," she tells him, dropping his bag and the blue folder on the table next to the door.

"Hear me?" His eyebrow raises as he looks at her. "What do you mean?"

"I want to hear you come for me," she says. "I don't want you to hold back like you did in the stairwell."

He grins. "There was someone sitting on the stairs," he reminds her. "I hardly dared to breathe too loudly."

She nods. "Exactly. I want to know what sounds you make when you aren't worried about being caught."

He looks around the windowless room, taking in the couch, the table surrounded by a few chairs, and the small black refrigerator pushed into the corner with an ancient microwave sitting on top of it. The microwave is so old that it has a turn dial; for a moment, William can't focus on anything else.

"It would be nice to not have to worry about someone walking in on us," he admits, then glances again at the microwave. "Doesn't that thing give you cancer?"

She chuckles, making her way over to him. "Probably. No one uses it anymore, but no one wants to carry it out of here and throw it away."

He nods, accepting her explanation. The college has lots of old things lingering in odd places, like the extra gym mats under the stairwell last night. He gives the room one more look. "How do you know no one will hear us in here? You can be quite loud."

"I was loud because the stairwell echoes," she says pertly, kneeling before him and taking his cock back into her hands. But then it's her turn to look at the microwave. "That thing is crazy loud, but when you're in the room out there, you can't hear it at all. We think it's because of the bookshelves." She thinks of the bookshelves that line the back wall of the Tutoring Center, filled with textbooks from all of the classes, shelves straining from the weight of all that paper.

William raises an eyebrow, watching as she leans down to lick the tip of his cock. "I thought you said no one used it."

She shrugs, then sucks him hard before releasing him just as abruptly. "Not anymore, I said. But we did a test run." She chuckles. "Like I said, it's dead around here at night—and we used to have two people on shift." She continues to slowly slide her hand up and down his shaft, a teasing rhythm.

"What happened?"

"Budget cuts, mostly. Eventually we will just close us up at 5 with everyone else, but for now, we follow the library schedule." She sighs, rolling her eyes as she recites: "Open until 8 so last minute students can get tutored."

"Does anyone ever come in at night?"

She shrugs, hands reaching up to unbutton the top few buttons of his shirt, and then she watches him tug it up over his head by grabbing the back of the neck in that magical way that men remove shirts. "Every now and then, but not regularly. And definitely not this time in the semester. Maybe around midterms and always more around finals, like they can just magically understand a semester's worth of work in an afternoon." She shrugs again. "I don't generally mind the empty hours. I find ways to entertain myself."

William smiles, watching her hands on his cock. "I see." She leans down to take him deep into her mouth again and he moans, low and slow. "You are going to leave yourself hanging if you keep doing that," he tells her, and she chuckles, the sound vibrating through his shaft as she releases him. She pauses long enough to unlace his boots and tug them off, then pulls his pants and boxers off. For the first time, William is completely naked. She takes a moment to appreciate the sight.

"I'd hate to leave myself hanging," she admits, but then leans forward to take his cock into her mouth for another few long lazy strokes, "but I do love to suck this cock."

"How would you like to fuck this cock?" he asks, pulling her up.

Kimberly giggles, "I thought you'd never ask." She climbs on to the couch, sliding her dress up as she settles herself on his lap, the warm heat between her thighs sliding around a little until she finds the tip of his cock and presses him against her. She moans, "Oh yes, that's nice," then slides the very tip inside her.

She pauses there, and William grabs her hips under the dress, sliding it up and over her head. Instead of tugging it completely off, though, he leaves it on her arms, and pulls both arms down over his head, trapping her on his lap with her hands wrapped in the dress behind his head. His hands return to the bare skin of her waist then, and he presses her down suddenly, his cock plunging deep inside of her, and she arches her back in pleasure, hands and arms straining against the dress holding her close to him. She moves as if to release herself, but he uses both arms to hold her close against him, setting a brisk rhythm with his hips.

"Oh no," he says into her neck, then uses one hand to pull her face down to his, his other hand still setting the rhythm on her hip, lips claiming hers with a fierce possession. "You are mine now," he tells her, sucking her lip in his excitement. She leans closer into him, body sliding up and down his cock, and he can feel the orgasm building, her pussy tightening around him, and then she cries out, and he smothers the sound with another passionate kiss, and she shudders against him.

"Fuck," she moans after he releases her mouth. "You are so good." She sits back as far as her dress will allow, then glances at him to see if he will release her arms.

"And you," he says, standing up in an athletic display, tugging her arms and the dress over his head, and flipping her so she lays beneath him on the couch, "are the loveliest thing I've ever seen." He stares down at her for a long moment, one knee on the couch and his other leg standing straight. He reaches forward to push her arms, still tangled in the dress, over her head, and presses them hard into the couch cushions before sliding his hand down her body, caressing her breasts and then sliding down to stroke her pussy again. "So wet for me," he tells her. "I want you to come again for me."

"Yes please," she agrees.

"Greedy girl," he says, then leans down to lick her clit, the motion sending a shudder through her body. "I want to watch you come again."

He licks again, burying his face against her, and then looks up the line of her body to see her face, eyes hooded with desire as she watches him. He reaches a hand up to hold a breast, and then her body is tightening, the orgasm rushing through her. "God yes!" she cries, then jerks away from him.

"Oh no," he insists, tugging her closer and settling a knee on the couch between her legs, leaning down so he can fuck her again. He lays his body on top of hers, hard cock plunging into her in one swift motion, and his other arm presses hard on her upraised arms, pinning her in place. "You wanted this cock?" he asks, hips moving fast and hard now. "You like this cock in your tight pussy?"

"Yes," she moans, body clinging to him, "Yes! Fuck me with your cock!"

He moves faster, harder, and she feels the pleasure rising in him with each stroke. "Come for me!" she screams, "Come in my pussy!" She wraps her legs around his hips, urging him on. "I want to hear you come!"

"Fuck yes!" William yells, burying himself in her in a few frantic strokes, and then he shudders with a wordless shout, body going taut above her. He manages a few more short jerky movements, then collapses on her, heart pounding against her chest so that the beat echoes in her skin. Kimberly lays there for a moment, enjoying the total bliss of complete satisfaction, and then she tries to take a deeper breath and is stopped by the weight on her chest. William seems to return to himself and lifts up on one elbow, relieving the pressure on her chest so she can breathe again, and she takes a deep breath.

"Wow," he mumbles, leaning toward the back of the couch to give her more room. He releases her arms and the dress, and scoots off to the side so he lays next to her on his side, his back pressed against the back of the couch. Kimberly brings her arms down with a groan and shucks off the remains of the dress, tossing it across the room to land on the floor. She reaches out to stroke his face, and then he leans down to kiss her, slow and languorous, enjoying the feel of her mouth without the demands of desire.

"I do hope that was sufficient entertainment," he says later, fingers lazily tracing circles around her nipples.

She smiles slowly, satisfaction and contentment evident in her expression. "Oh yes," she tells him. "I have to close early more often."

"And just think," he adds, "you didn't even get to read my story."

She raises an eyebrow. "Was it anything like this?"

He purses his lips. "Some yes. Some no." He trails a kiss along her neck and down to her nipple. "I want you to read it the next time you're her alone."

"You don't want me to read it to you?" she asks.

He shakes his head. "I did, originally, but it's far more fun to think of you reading it while you're here, thinking of me and all of the things I'm going to do to you."

She smiles up at him, "And will you be doing all of those things to me?"

He leans down to kiss her again, soft this time and burning with promise. "Oh yes. We still have to discuss the matter of your panties."

ALI WHIPPE

A li Whippe is the pen name of a professor in the higher education system who delights in imagining naughty distractions while enduring endless mind-numbing committee meetings. She loves to push the boundaries of the written word and the imagination, knowing that life at work would be way more exciting if more people didn't wear panties.

4 Horsemen Publications

Erotica

Dalia Lance
My Home on Whore Island
Slumming It on Slut Street
Training of the Tramp

72% Match

Ali Whippe
Office Hours
Tutoring Center

Honey Cummings
Sleeping with Sasquatch
Cuddling with Chupacabra
Naked with New Jersey Devil
Laying with the Lady in Blue
Wanton Woman in White
Beating it with Bloody Mary

Beau and Professor Bestialora
The Goat's Gruff
Goldie and Her Three Beards
Pied Piper's Pipe